How the Zebra Got Its Stripes

TALES FROM AROUND THE WORLD

By Justine and Ron Fontes

Illustrated by Peter Grosshauser

🌱 **A GOLDEN BOOK • NEW YORK**

Library of Congress Control Number: 2001090911

ISBN: 0-307-98870-8

www.goldenbooks.com

Printed in the United States of America   First Random House Edition 2003

20 19 18 17 16 15 14

"**G**reetings, nature lovers! I'm Professor Linus
Pinstripe on the trail of a mystery: How did the zebra
get its stripes?

"I'm here at a local watering hole on the plains of
Africa with some talkative creatures that say they
know the answer. Please tell us what you know,
Giraffe."

"Long ago," said Giraffe, "there were two kinds of zebras—the all-white kind and the all-black kind. The Black zebras could hide in the shadows when the lions came around. But the black zebras roasted in the hot sun. The white zebras felt cool, but they stood out like targets for the hungry lions."

"The zebras went to Wise Baboon for help. He gave the white zebras black paint. And he gave the black zebras white paint. Then the zebras went off to paint themselves.

"Now the once-black zebras felt cool, but they were targets for lions. And the once-white zebras could hide in the shadows, but they roasted in the hot sun."

"Once again, the zebras were upset. So they went back to Wise Baboon. This time, he gave them black-and-white striped paint. And zebras have been striped ever since."

"That is not the story my grandpa told me!" squawked Ostrich.

"Do go on, Ostrich," said Professor Pinstripe.

"Back in the beginning," said Ostrich, "zebras were as white as grubs! And zebras could run as swiftly as they do today."

"Once Zebra was safe from the leopard, it picked up its shredded shadow and said, 'From now on, my shadow will ride on me! That way it won't get torn again.' And that is how the zebra got its stripes."

"And, in case you're wondering how Zebra still casts a shadow on the ground, the answer is quite simple: Every morning when the sun comes up, we all get brand-new shadows."

Gazelle giggled. "You believe the silliest stories," she said. "I know how the zebra got its stripes."

"Please tell us," said Professor Pinstripe.

"Well," said Gazelle, "it happened on the day that the Creator held a party to celebrate the making of the world. Back then, Zebra was as tan as savanna grass and as lazy as a lion on a hot day."

"Wouldn't you know, Zebra slept right through the Creator's party! And when the Creator found Zebra asleep, he became very angry."

"'From now on,' said the Creator, 'you must wear your silly pajamas all the time!'

"In a flash, Zebra's striped pajamas turned into its skin! To this day, you can still see Zebra trotting and zigzagging in its striped pajamas."

"*Now* who's believing silly stories?" asked Lion, who had slinked up to the watering hole.

"What really happened was this," announced Lion. "In the first days of the world, the Creator was busy painting the animals different colors."

"Back then, Zebra was so ornery that the Creator had to paint Zebra through a cage. But just as the Creator started to paint, that cantankerous Zebra snorted!"

"The snorting sound startled the Creator, who tripped and spilled the bucket of white paint."

"Since half the paint fell on Zebra and the other half fell on the cage, Zebra ended up striped. But Zebra was so delighted with its new look that Zebra was never ornery again."

No one argued with Lion's story, because they had all sneaked away!
How do YOU think the zebra got its stripes?

SNEAKY STRIPES

No one really knows how the zebra got its stripes—or why!

The stripes probably help the zebra hide. Like a giraffe's spots or a soldier's camouflaged uniform, the zebra's stripes blur the shape of its body.

ARE YOU THERE, OR ARE YOU AIR?

Zebras are easy to see up close, of course. But when a lion or a leopard sees a zebra from far away, in the early morning or early evening light, the zebra's stripes look like wavy lines. These lines look like heat rising from the ground instead of a zebra.

CONFUSING MOVES

The zebra's stripes also help confuse a lion when it's choosing a zebra for dinner. As the lion moves in for the attack, a group of zebras rushes toward the lion. Suddenly, all the lion sees are stripes, not the zebra it wanted!

NO TWO ALIKE!

There may be another reason for the zebra's stripes: to allow zebras to recognize one another in large herds. Each zebra's striped pattern is as one-of-a-kind as a fingerprint!